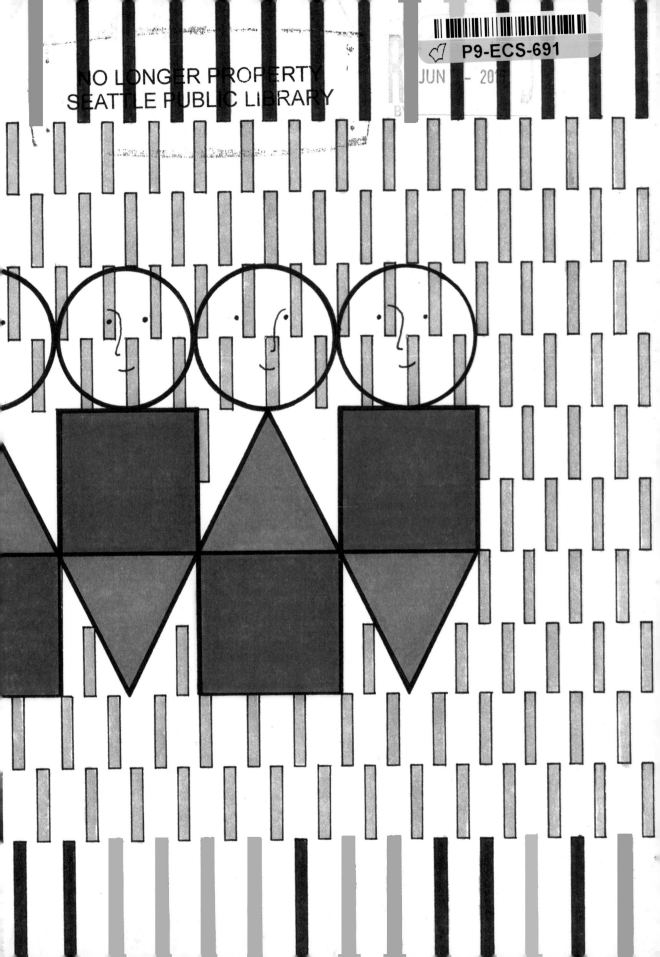

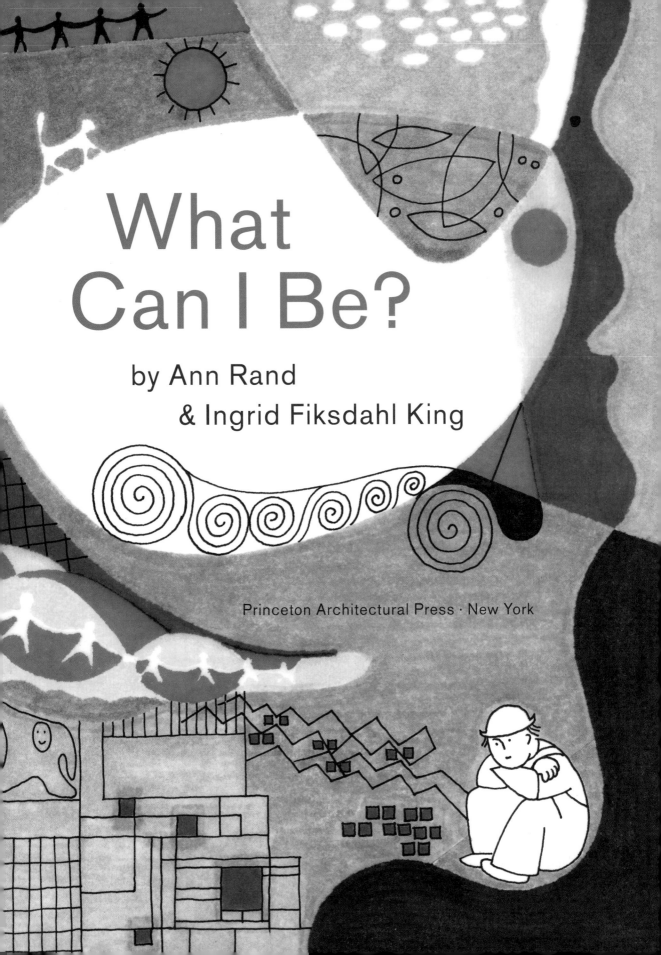

What Can I Be?

by Ann Rand
& Ingrid Fiksdahl King

Princeton Architectural Press · New York

and Ted and Ann and Mimi and Gina and Ethan and Eion and Franklin and Margaret and Mary and Judy and Hank and Ben and Hassan and Nathaniel and Bob and Gerald and Lily and Murphy and Keith and Nat and Harry and Matt and Marcia and Murray and Mary and Melissa and Susan and Marisa and Max and Jim and Saul and

...and for Catherine

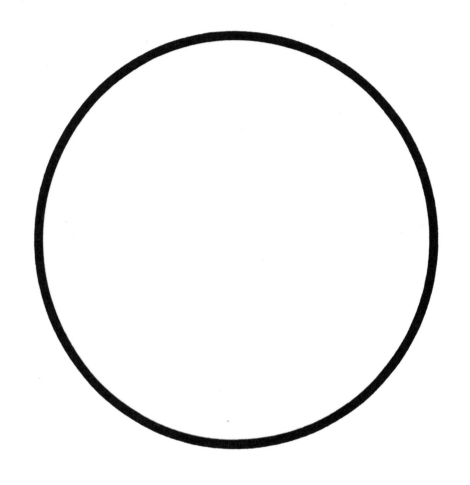

I'M ROUND

I'M RED

WHAT CAN I BE?

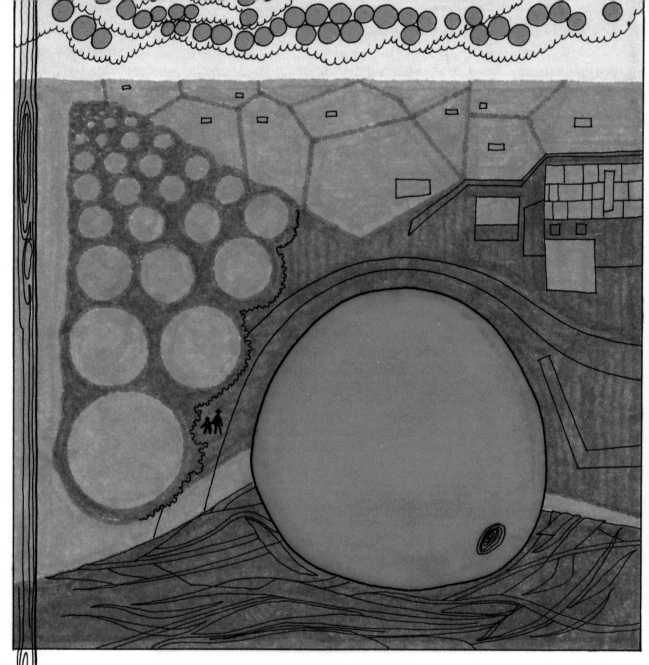

an apple that's ready to eat

or a | lollipop

or the sun before it sets
behind a high hilltop?

I'M ROUND

I'M RED

WHAT CAN YOU MAKE OF ME?

I'M THIN

OR THICK

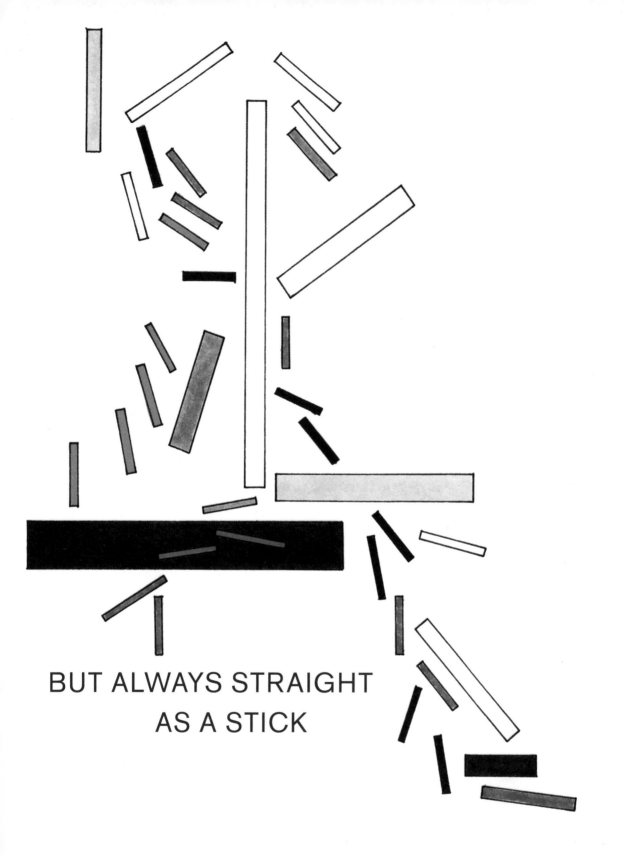

BUT ALWAYS STRAIGHT
AS A STICK

WHAT MIGHT I BE?

the mast of a ship

a jump   rope held tight...

the trunk
of a very young tree

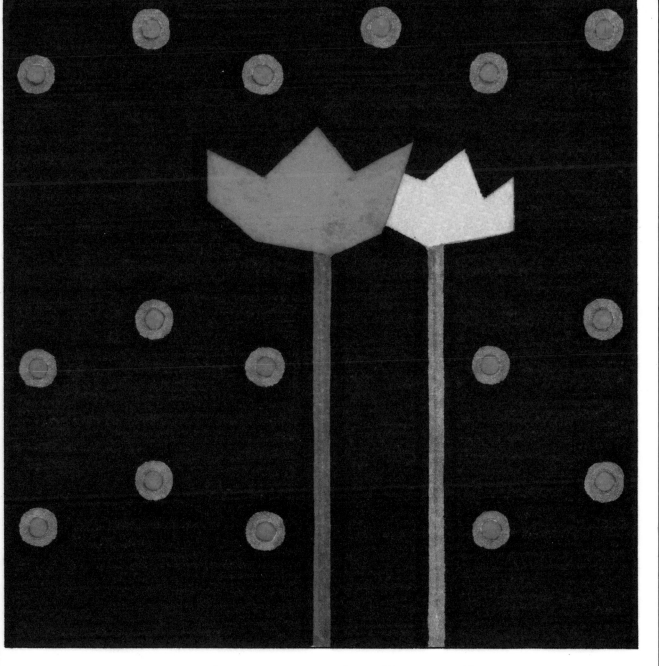

or the stem of a flower?

THERE ARE A HUNDRED THINGS
YOU COULD MAKE OF ME

I'M BLUE

I'M SQUARE

WHAT IS THERE
    THAT YOU CAN MAKE OF ME?

a little door for a cat

or a dog?

the top of a box?

or window panes
that look onto the sky?

NOW YOU TRY...

WHAT ELSE CAN I BE?

IF I'M A LINE THAT'S NOT STRAIGHT

IF I WOBBLE AND WEAVE

WHAT COULD I BE?

I can easily make

a splendid snake

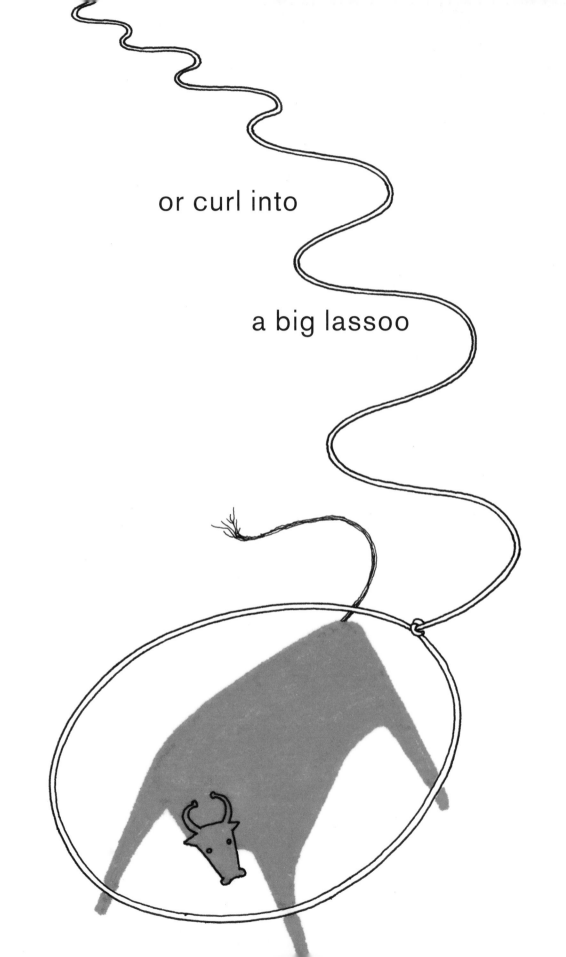

or curl into

a big lassoo

I could be the ruffled edge
     of waves
          on a stormy sea

BUT NOW LET'S SEE
WHAT YOU CAN DO WITH ME

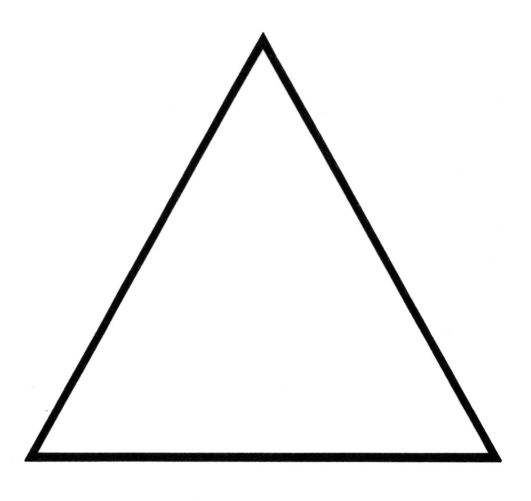

I'M A TRIANGLE

I'M GREEN

I COULD BE . . .

a
Christmas
tree

the sail of a boat

a tent

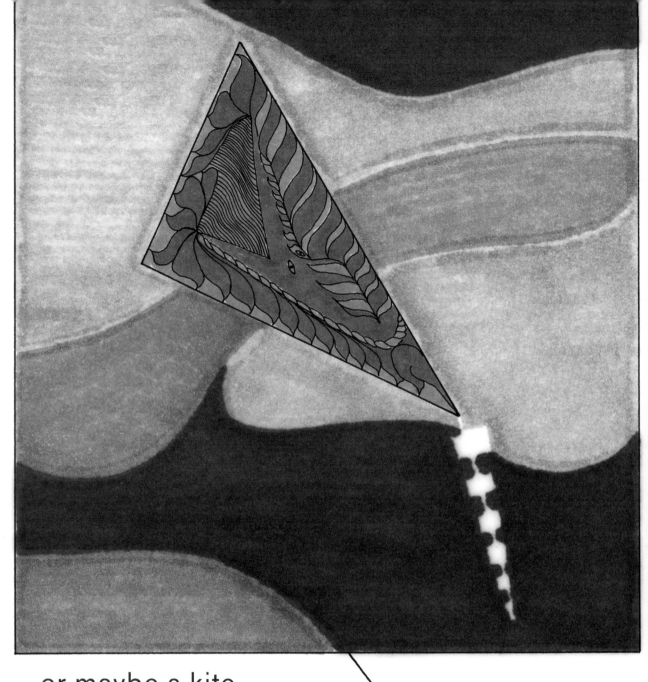

or maybe a kite
flying high
in a windblown sky

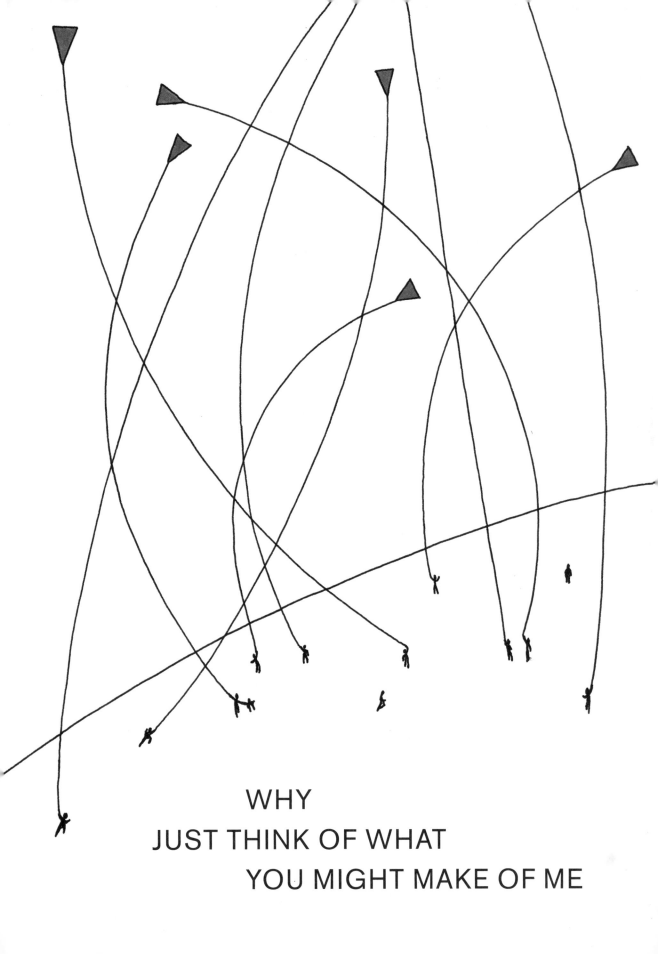

WHY
JUST THINK OF WHAT
YOU MIGHT MAKE OF ME

LET'S SAY I'M ANY SHAPE
OR COLOR

AND ONE THING I VERY OFTEN DO
IS FOLLOW YOU AROUND

a toy engine on a string

or a puppy you just found?

there are so many things

that I could be

WE'LL HAVE TO WAIT
AND SEE
JUST WHAT YOU MAKE OF ME

Published by
Princeton Architectural Press
A McEvoy Group company
37 East Seventh Street
New York, New York 10003

Visit our website at www.papress.com

© 2016 Ann Rand Ozbekhan
Illustrations © 2016 Ingrid Fiksdahl King
All rights reserved
Printed and bound in China
19 18 17 16   First Edition

ISBN 978-1-61689-472-6

Special thanks to: Nicola Bednarek Brower, Janet Behning,
Erin Cain, Tom Cho, Benjamin English, Jenny Florence,
Jan Cigliano Hartman, Lia Hunt, Mia Johnson, Valerie Kamen,
Simone Kaplan-Senchak, Stephanie Leke, Diane Levinson,
Jennifer Lippert, Sarah McKay, Jaime Nelson Noven, Rob Shaeffer,
Sara Stemen, Paul Wagner, Joseph Weston, and Janet Wong
of Princeton Architectural Press —Kevin C. Lippert, publisher

Library of Congress Cataloging-in-Publication Data
available upon request

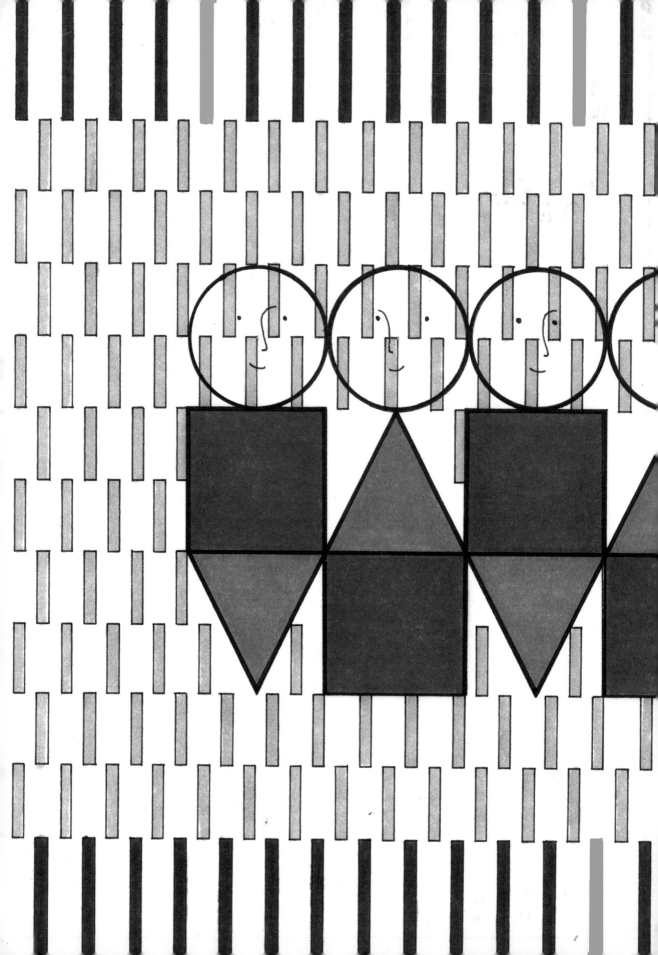